Alice
and the
Garden

Written and Illustrated
by Anna Johnston

ISBN: 978-1-09832-254-0

For Adam, who always eats his greens.

Chapter 1
The Broccoli

Alice was staring down the last two broccoli trees on her plate as she heard her trusty partner in crime take position beneath her chair.

Ash, the family pup, sat at attention as Alice placed her napkin skillfully over the larger broccoli piece.

Her parents were distracted with her squirming little brother, struggling to sit still across the table.

In one swipe, she picked the napkin off the table and dropped the broccoli to the floor. In the blink of an eye, Ash gobbled it up.

Alice pushed the remaining little broccoli tree into position on the plate.

It was bright green, with a dark leafy top.

She wrinkled her nose.

With a swift movement, she placed her napkin on top.

Her father turned back his attention to her.

"What a great job finishing your dinner, Alice! All that broccoli calls for dessert."

Alice was in the clear.

Until... Little brother Louie fumbled and dropped his fork. Eyes frozen wide, Alice watched it tumble to the ground beside her.

As her mother leaned under the table to pick up the fork, she gasped as she met eyes with Ash and the pile of half eaten broccoli under Alice.

With her tail between her legs, Ash ran to her dog bed in the other room, leaving Alice on her own to face her parents.

"Alice Marie!"

Chapter 2
The Plan

That night, as Alice lay in bed, she pouted thinking about the untouched cookies sitting on the kitchen counter.

Vegetables always seemed to get in the way of her dessert. She hatched a plan to get rid of them all.

The next day, Alice waited until the kitchen was empty. Giving Ash the signal, she tiptoed in with her red wagon behind her.

She gathered all of the vegetables that would make it to her plate that week. Just to be safe, she grabbed the lemons, unsure if they were vegetables or not.

Once her wagon was piled high, she turned to the back door to make a dash to the outdoor trash cans.

Then she heard footsteps behind her.

"Alice Marie!"

Alice looked over her shoulder to see her parents walking towards her, shaking their heads at Alice and the overflowing wagon.

One by one, Alice put away the funny looking fennel, the heavy purple cabbage, and the juicy red tomatoes as her father watched over her with arms crossed. The fridge was filled to the brim once again.

"Now," he said."I want you to see where those vegetables came from. Miss Mindy next door has spent all season growing her garden, and I don't think she'd like to hear that her beautiful produce almost made its way to the trash can."

Chapter 3
The Garden

That afternoon, Alice's father walked her over to Miss Mindy's house.

From Alice's bedroom, if she climbed onto the window sill, she could see the green vines spiraling out from Miss Mindy's yard. Sometimes she saw squirrels enjoying a ripe tomato on the fence. Butterflies made appearances, their bright colors flittering across the sea of green. Life seemed to flock to Miss Mindy's garden.

But this was the first time she had been invited into the thick jungle of plants. Alice was in awe as she saw the rows of climbing vines and lush leaves.

It was just like the magical gardens in her favorite fairytales.

Then she finally spotted Miss Mindy, hidden behind the cucumber vines on her hands and knees.

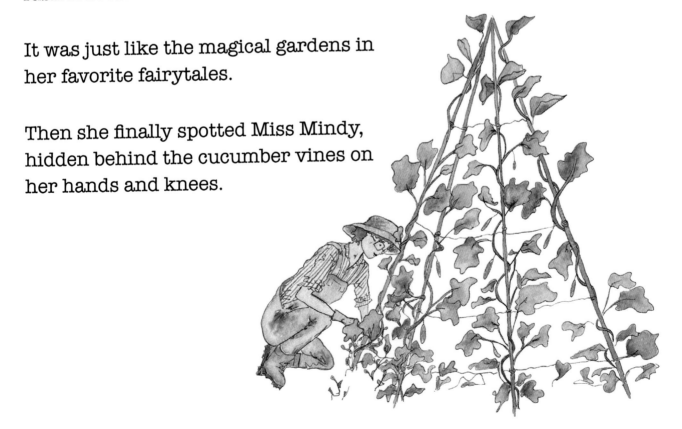

Alice eyed Miss Mindy's dirty overalls and gloves.

Alice's tutu was not meant for gardening, but she didn't know that
cucumbers grew on vines, so she made her way to get a closer
look. Alice thought that cucumbers came in a bag at the store, or
sometimes in a box from the farmers market.

As she looked around, all the different colors and shapes and sizes of
the vegetables around her came into view.

Miss Mindy, following her gaze, started to name all of the different
produce growing around them.

Eggplant, cucumber, zucchini, string bean, radish, tomato, and
lettuce.

They grew in long rows, and Miss Mindy had to point under the
zucchini plants' wide leaves for Alice to see the slender little zucchini
bodies.

"How come there's so many colors? I thought plants were just green," Alice asked.

"The colors are the plants' power!

Just like they protect each unique plant, our bodies need all of the different colors to help us stay healthy and strong."

Miss Mindy then held up two onions - one red and one white.

"Which one do you think is more powerful for us to eat?"

Alice examined the rich, deep color of the red onion, and pointed to that one with confidence.

"Yes!" exclaimed Miss Mindy.

"When you look at your plate at every meal, do you see a rainbow?"

Alice thought back to her lunch that day, and she remembered her red raspberries and yellow pineapple. But then her mind turned to blue frosted cupcakes.

As Miss Mindy taught Alice the powers of each plant color, Alice quickly realized that eating her favorite cupcake frosting wasn't the same as eating living plants.

"What's that?" asked Alice, pointing to the strong smelling pile on the asparagus patch.

"That is compost." explained Miss Mindy, "Every living thing has nutrients and power. We can use what's left of our meals to bring the soil life. The plants feed off of the rich soil to make our vegetables strong and delicious. What you see here, Alice, is the circle of life. Isn't it magical?"

Magic.

That's what Alice needed to master her favorite tree in the backyard. Ever since her last birthday, she had been trying to reach the top. She was determined to one day be big and strong enough to climb it.

That would show her parents she was finally ready for a treehouse.

"Miss Mindy, what in your garden will make my bones and muscles strong?" asked Alice.

"My favorite vegetables are leafy greens, like kale, spinach, and lettuce. These beautiful leaves provide calcium for your bones and fiber for your body. They are the most powerful in my garden, except of course for my herbs."

Chapter 4
The Herbs

The herb garden was set on the sun kissed edge of Miss Mindy's yard. Miss Mindy brushed her fingers across the lavender, rosemary, and thyme, releasing a relaxing scent across the garden.

She cut a handful of dill, and then guided Alice to a small table. Slicing a cucumber from her garden haul, Miss Mindy sprinkled a pinch of salt and placed a piece of dill on top of the cucumber sliver before handing it to Alice.

"Not only do herbs make any meal extra delicious, they each contain unique powers that heal and strengthen." said Miss Mindy.

With a breath, Alice closed her eyes and took a bite.

In that bite, she tasted the garden. The soil, the sun, and the tender care that Miss Mindy gave her plants.

When her father returned to thank Miss Mindy and bring Alice home, he was shocked to hear that Alice willingly ate cucumber. With a wink, Miss Mindy handed him a packet of seeds and a basket filled to the brim of his favorites, including extra leafy greens to help Alice grow big and strong.

As her parents put away the fresh produce in the kitchen, Alice sat on the floor and drew her dream treehouse, covered in green vines.

That night, Alice curled up with Ash on the couch and told her about her day in the magical garden.

"I pinky promise I will eat two green vegetables and one red fruit tomorrow."

Alice gave Ash a squeeze, and smiled knowing she'd have to share some of her leafy greens.

the end.